To Elizabeth (Betty) Hogan – a wonderful grandmother with a sharp wit, creative mind and a talent for making beautiful things
Carlie

For the young fashionista in our family, Tilly xxxx
Tamsin

Published by Allen & Unwin in 2018

Copyright © Text, Carlie Gibson 2018
Copyright © Illustrations, Tamsin Ainslie 2018

Allen & Unwin – Australia
83 Alexander Street,
Crows Nest NSW 2065,
Australia
Phone: (61 2) 8425 0100
Email: info@allenandunwin.com
Web: www.allenandunwin.com

A catalogue record for this book is available from the National Library of Australia.
catalogue.nla.gov.au

ISBN (AUS) 978 1 76052 364 0
ISBN (UK) 978 1 91163 135 4

Cover and text design by Julia Eim
Colour reproduction by Splitting Image, Clayton, Victoria
This book was printed in July 2018 by C&C Offset Printing Co. Ltd, China

10 9 8 7 6 5 4 3 2 1

the Sisters Saint-Claire
and the
Royal Mouse Ball

Carlie Gibson
and
Tamsin Ainslie

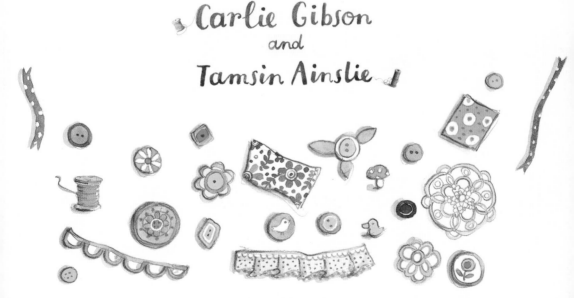

ALLEN&UNWIN
SYDNEY · MELBOURNE · AUCKLAND · LONDON

$\mathcal{T}$his is the tale of the Sisters Saint-Claire
Who lived with their parents, Odette and Pierre
Harriet, Violet, Beatrice, Minette
And little Cecile, we must not forget!

Harriet loved all the second-hand stores
She looked for old treasures to fill up her drawers
In Thistle Do's Thrift Shop she found such a treat
A red velvet coat worn by Dame Marguerite!

Violet was putting her money away
To visit the city of Paris one day
She'd dress in her finest and wander the streets
Shopping while eating Parisian treats

Beatrice Saint-Claire had a weakness for shoes
At Louis Crouton's she would stop and peruse
She picked out some sandals to match her best dress
Then looked for a place she could buy them for less

Minette, still agog in Miss Must-Have-It's store
Had saved all her cash for a few months or more
She looked in her purse and let out a squeak
'At last, I can buy a fur crimper this week!'

Cecile Saint-Claire was a young fashionista
Wearing the clothes handed down from each sister

Buttons and brooches were added with passion
Turning old clothes into new season's fashion

The girls scurried swiftly back home to Mama
Then danced arm-in-arm 'round the room with Papa
He bowed most politely, then reached in his coat
And handed the sisters a fine royal note

To all the Saint-Claires
You are hereby invited
to join me this Sunday
I'd be most delighted!
Dress in your best
for a Royal Mouse Ball
I'll open the palace for mice
one and all!

Sincerely
HRH Queen Julie S Cheeser

Hattie looked down at her second-hand dress
While Violet was twirling her beads in distress

'I'm sorry,' said Beatrice, 'I'm not being mean
But none of our outfits are right for the Queen.'

Pierre spoke with passion: 'The Queen will not care!
Your style is unique – you're the Sisters Saint-Claire!'

'Please,' begged Cecile, 'Can we go? Can we go?'
But Hattie refused: 'We'll politely say no.'

The sisters wrote back to the palace that day
And when the Queen read it, she sat in dismay

All mice had replied with the very same line
'We thank you, but sadly, we have to decline.'

The Queen sat alone for a moment or two
And asked herself quietly, 'What should I do?'
She picked up the note from the Sisters Saint-Claire
Then ran for the door with her tail in the air

Her guards shouted out as they ran close behind
'We'll fetch you the carriage – we really don't mind!'

She knocked on a door with a right royal rap
Odette was aghast and Pierre in a flap!

The Queen smiled warmly, her arms open wide
'My friends, the Saint-Claires, may I please come inside?'

She looked at the little house filled with old wares
No fine things in sight, but such treasure was theirs!
She let out a sigh as she sipped on some tea
'The only mouse coming this Sunday ... is me!'

'Your life looks so glamorous,' Hattie replied
'It is,' said the Queen, 'but it's lonely inside.'
'Your Highness,' said Beatrice, 'while mice are quite loyal
Perhaps they're afraid to dress up for a royal.'

The sisters, they chittered and chattered aloud . . .
Minette said, 'We'll help you to bring in the crowd!
Send a new letter and ask every mouse
To make their own outfit from things in their house!'

The Queen hugged the sisters. 'It's brilliant!' she cried
'We'll help you to make one as well,' they replied

'We must go at once to our grand-maman's place!'

The Queen, out in front, set a blistering pace

Knitting and sewing were Grand-maman's passion
She kept squares of fabric to match any fashion
'With patterns and scissors, a needle and cotton
You'll all have an outfit that's never forgotten!'

They looked through the dress-up box under the stairs
And cut up old curtains and sheets into squares

Minette and Cecile pinned the patterns in place
While Beatrice was helping the Queen add some lace

Hattie and Violet were sewing with care
Till show-stopping outfits were ready to wear

On Sunday, the guards threw the doors open wide
A jazz quartet played in the garden outside

Ladies and gentlemice showed style and passion
Proudly displaying their home-crafted fashion

Louis Crouton had a red tartan suit.

Dame Marguerite wore a hat made of fruit!

Pierre wore culottes with a vest and a shirt.

Odette turned a peacock print into a skirt.

Harriet, Violet, Beatrice, Minette
And little Cecile, we must not forget
Arrived at the Royal Mouse Ball with the Queen
Who shone in a fabulous pantsuit of green!

She looked at the crowd and exclaimed with delight
'You're here, every one of you! Oh, what a sight!'

They danced 'round the room, every mouse taking part

Until the Queen spoke to them, straight from the heart

'I live in a palace and wear a fine crown

'I glisten and sparkle in each evening gown

'I sit at a table where food never ends

But all of it feels rather dull without friends

'I welcome you all to my home with such pleasure

'You shine so much brighter than all of its treasure!'

Finger Puppets

You can make your own Sisters Saint-Claire with a few simple supplies! Make sure you ask an adult for some help as you'll be using scissors and a needle.

WHAT YOU WILL NEED

Felt squares in 3 different colours – try grey, white and pink
A medium-sized needle
Cotton thread in different colours – try grey, brown and pink
A pen or pencil

HOW TO MAKE YOUR FINGER PUPPET

UN.
Place your pointer finger on one of the felt squares. Trace around your finger with a pen or pencil, leaving some room either side to stitch it together later. Take your finger off the felt and draw some ears on either side.

DEUX.
Cut out your mouse shape, including the ears (don't cut them off!). Lay your first mouse shape on the same felt and trace around it. Then cut out your second mouse shape. Put the two shapes together with the pencil marks facing each other. Using a needle and cotton thread, stitch around the outside of the mouse shape. Make sure you don't sew the bottom edge – this is where you will put your puppet on your finger.

TROIS.
Using a different coloured felt, draw two small circles for inside the ears, and another to make the face. Cut them out carefully. Stitch or glue them onto your mouse shape.

QUATRE.
Stitch a nose, then two eyes and some whiskers.

You can add anything you like to your mouse to make it your own.
Try a crown, a scarf or even some sequins.

Magnifique!